D1207354

By Don M. Winn
Illustrated by Dave Allred

OTHER CARDBOARD BOX ADVENTURES BOOKS BY DON WINN

Chipper the Clown

Chipper and the Unicycle

The Tortoise and the Hairpiece

The Incredible Martin O'Shea

Shelby the Cat

Twitch the Squirrel and the Forbidden Bridge

The Watch Cat

The Higgledy-Piggledy Pigeon

Available in hardcover, softcover and eBook formats

www.donwinn.com

Take the stories to the next level with interactive versions from InteractBooks.

www.interactbooks.com

Superhero Special Hardcover Edition
ISBN: 978-1-937615-13-0
Copyright © 2010 by Don M. Winn

Published by Cardboard Box Adventures
www.donwinn.com

This book is dedicated to my dad, the greatest hero of my youth,
who was always there when I needed him the most.

HOW TO USE THIS BOOK:

Cardboard Box Adventures books are books worth talking about. They are designed to give parents and children an opportunity to have meaningful discussions about important topics. The stories are just the beginning. Please read them aloud together and then use the questions included at the end of the stories to begin conversations with your children. Many of the questions will help you to see how well your child understood the story. Others will help you and your children talk about what's on their minds and what's important to them. The last section of questions is designed to help kids become active thinkers, inspiring their creativity and imaginations.

INTRODUCTION:

What is a hero? In comic books and movies, heroes sometimes have some kind of amazing power that they use to help other people. But real heroes are ordinary people that do ordinary things to help others. If you can find a way to help someone who really needs your help, you will always be a hero to that person.

Most of the time, the ordinary people doing ordinary things to help us are the most important people in our lives. With this idea of a hero in mind, I can't think of a greater hero than a loving parent.

I give you Superhero!

It was just another average day,
I hadn't time for school or play,
a hero's call I must obey,
a Superhero, I!

With super ears I hear the call,
there's panic at the city mall,
it's up to me to save them all,
a Superhero, I!

At fighting crime I am an ace,
I wear a mask to hide my face,
with super speed I'm on the case,
a Superhero, I!

With my super strength and x-ray eyes,
all crooks will soon meet their demise,
it matters not a hero's size,
a Superhero, I!

A beanstalk giant I just beat,
the big bad wolf met with defeat,
so what new villain will I meet?
A Superhero, I!

Stopped in my tracks at Tenth and Green,
where frightened crowds ran from the scene,
I wondered what this sight could mean,
a Superhero, I!

While waiting for the smoke to clear,
two villains just ahead appear,
unwanted DREAD and evil FEAR!
A Superhero, I!

These villains I have seen before,
they're feelings all of us abhor,
and now they're back
to scare some more,
a Superhero, I!

Before the villains I could scold,
DREAD quickly turned my body cold,
as FEAR confined me in its hold,
a Superhero, I!

They're not like any other foe,
they have a red and orange glow,
the more I'm scared, the more they grow,
a Superhero, I!

Each step I tried to make was slow,
I couldn't stay, but couldn't go,
my super strength now ceased to flow,
a Superhero, I!

Against these foes I can't contend,
but there's one hero that won't bend,
a call for help I try to send,
a Superhero, I!

Just then I woke upon my bed,
my dad was standing overhead,
then FEAR soon left as well as DREAD,
a Superhero, I!

For in defeat I will not fall,
when there's a hero I can call,
the greatest hero of them all,
it is my dad, not I!

Questions Parents Can Discuss With Their Children

1. What is a hero?

2. Do you need to have super powers to be a hero?

3. How was the dad in this story a hero to his son?

4. How could you be a hero?

5. Who is your greatest hero and why?

QUESTIONS FOR ACTIVE THINKING

1. What do you imagine is Superhero's favorite color? His favorite place to play? His favorite book? His favorite food? What kind of sports do you imagine he is good at? What is his school like?

2. Do you remember a time in your family when someone saved the day by doing ordinary things?

3. What sort of super things would you like to do when you are older? What sort of super things would you like to do now? Did you do anything super today? Why?

4. Has anyone ever helped you feel better after you had a scary dream? What could you do to help someone else feel better who had a scary dream?

5. What is something amazing you would do if you had imaginary superhero powers? What is something amazing you could do without any imaginary superhero powers? Write or tell a story or draw a picture about both questions.

6. Can you think of a time when someone took care of you when you were scared? How did it make you feel to know that you were cared for?

7. Do you think anyone at Superhero's school knows about his secret identity? How do they find out?

ABOUT THE AUTHOR

Don Winn has been writing since 1998. He started by writing poetry and then moved on to writing rhyming children's picture books. He is surprised that he likes to write so much because he remembers that when he was in school, he would do anything he could to avoid writing. Don Winn lives in Round Rock, Texas, with his wife and two cats.

Don Winn is the author of the Cardboard Box Adventures series of children's picture books, which includes the titles *The Tortoise and the Hairpiece, The Higgledy-Piggledy Pigeon, Superhero, Chipper the Clown, Chipper and the Unicycle, The Incredible Martin O'Shea, Twitch the Squirrel and the Forbidden Bridge, The Watch Cat*, and *Shelby the Cat*.

Visit his website at www.donwinn.com for more information and all the latest news.

ABOUT CARDBOARD BOX ADVENTURES

Don Winn calls his series of books Cardboard Box Adventures because he remembers how much fun he had as a child using his imagination while playing with a simple cardboard box. The box could be anything he wanted it to be: a spaceship, a cave, a fort, a submarine...the possibilities were endless!

Some of his other favorite memories involve the times his grandmother would read aloud to him and talk about what they had read together. He is grateful to her for doing this because he knows now that it always reassured him of her love for him and her interest in his thoughts and feelings.

With his books, Don hopes to fuel kids' active imaginations, share some helpful object lessons, and provide opportunities for parents and children to reinforce their loving bond through conversations about important topics.

CPSIA information can be obtained at www.ICGtesting.com
Printed in the USA
LVIW01n1028050415
433358LV00006B/18